CHOOSE YOUR OWN ADVENTURE®
titles in Large-Print Editions:

All-Time Best-Sellers!

CHOOSE YOUR OWN ADVENTURE® • 110

INVADERS FROM WITHIN

BY EDWARD PACKARD

ILLUSTRATED BY FRANK BOLLE

Gareth Stevens Publishing
MILWAUKEE

For a free color catalog describing Gareth Stevens' list of high-quality books, call 1-800-542-2595 (USA) or 1-800-461-9120 (Canada). Gareth Stevens' Fax: (414) 225-0377.

Library of Congress Cataloging-in-Publication Data

Packard, Edward.
    Invaders from within/by Edward Packard; illustrated by
Frank Bolle.
       p. cm. — (Choose your own adventure; 110)
      Summary: The reader's decisions control the course of an adventure
involving a glowing mountaintop dome that may be from outer space.
    ISBN 0-8368-1401-0
    1. Plot-your-own stories. [1. Unidentified flying objects—Fiction.
2. Extraterrestrial beings—Fiction.   3.   Science fiction.
4. Plot-your-own stories.] I. Bolle, Frank, ill. II. Title. III. Series.
PZ7.P1245In   1995
[Fic]—dc20   95-366

This edition first published in 1995 by
Gareth Stevens Publishing
1555 North RiverCenter Drive, Suite 201
Milwaukee, Wisconsin 53212 USA

CHOOSE YOUR OWN ADVENTURE® is a trademark of Bantam Doubleday Dell Books for Young Readers, a division of Bantam Doubleday Dell Publishing Group, Inc.

Original conception of Edward Packard.
Interior illustrations by Frank Bolle. Cover art by David Mattingly.

Printed in the United States of America

1 2 3 4 5 6 7 8 9 99 98 97 96 95

INVADERS
FROM WITHIN

WARNING!!!

Do not read this book straight through from beginning to end. These pages contain many different adventures that you may have when you encounter a strange, alien force. From time to time as you read along, you will be asked to make a choice. Your choice may lead to success or disaster!

The adventures you have are the results of your choices. You are responsible because you choose! After you make a choice, follow the instructions to see what happens to you next.

Think carefully before you make a decision. While hiking on Hawk Mountain you might experience a temporary loss of memory. Your suspicion that aliens from space are responsible could be true, but your adventure may turn out to be more dangerous than exciting. Even if you do manage to solve the mystery of Hawk Mountain, you may not like what you find out.

Good luck!

1

You're standing on Hawk Mountain, near Table Rock Spring. Although it's just about the most peaceful place in the world, you've never been so flustered in all your life! A moment ago it was midday, the sun shining bright overhead; but now suddenly you notice that the sun is behind the ridge, and darkness is about to fall.

Somehow time has passed, as if you've fallen asleep. The entire afternoon has gone by without your realizing it. The thing is, you're certain that you *didn't* fall asleep!

For the past two weeks, you've been visiting your uncle Howard and your aunt Nan in northern California, working part-time on their ranch. You're having a lot of fun. However, the summer is almost over. School will be starting up again in less than a week, and soon you'll be going home.

This morning you hiked up to Table Rock with Dusty, the family dog. When you got there, you drank some water out of the clear spring that runs out from under the rock you are sitting on. That's the last thing you can remember!

Your aunt and uncle must be worried about you. You've got to start heading home. The sky has clouded over, and there is no moon out to guide you. You grab your backpack and call out, "Dusty, where are you, you dumb mutt?"

Turn to page 2.

Dusty is nowhere in sight, which is surprising—it's not like him to take off without you. He's a big, strong dog, part Newfoundland and part German shepherd. He's not really a dumb mutt. For years you've been visiting the ranch during summer vacation, and you and Dusty are great pals.

It's getting late—you've got to find him. You strap on your backpack and start heading down the trail.

You take only a few steps when you see Dusty. He's sniffing the ground, his front legs pawing the dirt. "Dusty!" you call.

He jerks his head and gives you a strange look. Then he shakes his body, just as he does when he comes out of the water.

"Come on, boy, we've no time to waste. We've got to get back home." You slap your thigh a couple of times, indicating that he should follow you. Then you continue on down the trail.

Minutes later the two of you reach a narrow ledge where the trail skirts along the edge of a cliff. It's really dangerous—a single misstep could send you plunging down the eight-hundred-foot face of the mountain.

As you traverse the ledge, you pick your steps carefully. You'd be up on the mountain all night if Dusty wasn't along with you. Though it is too dark to see, he knows how to find the trail. Even so, it's pitch-dark and almost nine o'clock when you and Dusty finally walk in the kitchen door of your uncle's ranch house.

Go on to the next page.

You find your uncle Howard and your aunt Nan waiting up for you, sipping tea at the kitchen table. With them is Jeb, the ranch foreman. When you explain to them what happened to you—how several hours seemed to disappear out of the day—your uncle Howard just gives you a skeptical look. Your aunt Nan comes over and runs her palm across your forehead. "I'm afraid you're coming down with a fever," she says. "That must be why you slept so long."

"But I didn't fall asleep," you insist. "One moment it was the afternoon, the next thing I knew it was a lot later!"

"That's the tallest story I've ever heard," your uncle says. "I'm really surprised at you."

You're about to reply in your defense when Jeb says, "Don't be so sure it's a made-up story, Howard. I recall hearing a few months back about a young couple that went up to Table Rock for a picnic lunch on a Tuesday afternoon. Well, sir, when they returned it was Wednesday, and they didn't even know it was the next day. People said it must have been some kind of food poisoning. But I've been thinking. It strikes me it was something else. Maybe, just maybe, it has something to do with aliens from outer space."

"I think it has something to do with the water from the spring," you say. "I drank from it just before I lost track of the time, and Dusty did, too."

Turn to page 10.

4

As you drive west toward Steamboat Springs, the professor brings you up-to-date on his research. "Steamboat Springs was given its name because of a natural spring or geyser that once existed there that made a sound like a steamboat—at least that's what I've been told. In any event, there are a number of springs remaining in the area. The ones we'll be visiting are often used for swimming by those lucky enough to know about them. The water is so warm you can bathe there even in the winter."

"It sounds like a good place for alien creatures to gestate," you say.

"One would think so," he says. "The water there at one time used to be as pure as any in the world. I don't know how it is now, however. Steamboat Springs has become a big ski resort, and with all the condos they've built on the side of the mountain, there's bound to be some pollution."

"What I've been wondering," you say, "is how we're going to keep from passing out and losing our memories? If we do get to see a power dome, how are we going to remember that we saw it?"

"I think Dr. Vivaldi has worked that out," Professor Burns replies.

Go on to the next page.

"That's right," says Dr. Vivaldi. "As you know, human brains work on electrical energy. It is my belief that these aliens have been sending out highly focused electrical waves that are able to erase short-term memory for several hours. I think we can counter this effect by wearing these helmets that I have designed. They are lined with electrical insulation. Here, I've brought one along for each of us."

Turn to page 51.

6

You get out an old blanket and make a nest for Slimy in an unused chicken coop outside the workroom. You put a bowl of water and a bowl of milk next to it, plus a small dish of tuna fish, some lettuce, and a little hamburger that you find in the house. You figure it ought to like at least one of those things.

Unfortunately the alien refuses to eat or drink anything. It just sort of crouches into itself, moving its two antenna-like trunks back and forth. Looking out the window, you see a station wagon pulling up the driveway. Your aunt and uncle are back from the movies, and you run out to tell them about Slimy.

Needless to say, they're amazed by your discovery. They give you a number of suggestions about what to do with the creature, but you figure you know as much as anyone does in a case like this. You decide to keep an eye on it for a while, and try a number of different foods until you find out what it likes best.

Turn to page 33.

8

You decide to bring Dusty along. As you climb the mountain trail, you get increasingly nervous. Dusty seems nervous, too. The moon keeps ducking behind big, fast-moving clouds, and sometimes it's too dark to see the ground under your feet. It's almost one in the morning when you reach the dangerous intersection where the trail crosses a narrow ledge on the steepest face of the mountain.

You work your way slowly along the ledge. Dusty is right behind you, but you shoo him back a little, afraid he'll trip you up. Soon you're safely off the ledge. You relax a moment, then continue on a few hundred feet farther until you come to a bend in the trail. In the fuzzy light of the moon you can see the dim silhouette of Table Rock. The spring gushes out of the base of the rock, and a little rivulet flows from the pool of water beneath it.

You walk through the lush, damp grass near the spring, looking for clues. Dusty, meanwhile, is sniffing furiously at something a few feet away. Suddenly he starts digging, sending up tufts of wet grass and mud.

You watch until he gets tired and gives up, then you walk over and examine the area he's dug. Nothing seems out of the ordinary, when suddenly you hear a strange sound coming from underneath your feet. You jump back in a hurry, certain that there's going to be an earthquake! A few yards away from you, a round, ten-foot patch of earth splits open.

Turn to page 54.

You try to get Dr. Vivaldi's attention, but she's nowhere in sight. You fix your eyes again on the power dome, wondering if it extends underground or if it is just sitting on the surface. You walk slowly toward it, hoping your helmet will protect you, even at close range.

You move closer and closer, like a cat stalking a bird. When you're only a few feet away, you feel a tingling sensation in your head, but curiosity drives you on. Soon you're close enough to touch the curved wall of light before you.

The power dome looks even stranger up close than it does from a distance. You wonder what's inside. You have the feeling you could pass your hand right through it!

Slowly you move your hand closer to the strange, luminous surface. You feel no heat, but you do feel a strong tingling in your fingers.

If you touch the power dome you might get a radiation burn, or worse. You're intensely curious to learn everything you can about this strange object and find out what exactly it is, but perhaps you should step back and get the others.

*If you touch the glowing dome,
turn to page 58.*

If you back away, turn to page 103.

Aunt Nan stands with her hands on her hips, a puzzled look on her face. "Why, that's ridiculous. That's supposed to be the purest water in California. A while ago people were talking about bottling it and selling it in the supermarkets."

"I don't see how—" you start to say.

"It's like they say," your uncle Howard interrupts, shaking his head. "Pollution's getting in everywhere these days. Maybe that's why the deal fell through."

"Hummph. Pollution wouldn't cause someone to pass out and sleep the day away. I still say it's a fever," your aunt Nan says, feeling your forehead once again.

"Well, I don't know what to make of all this," your uncle Howard says. "But it's late. I think we better turn in."

That night you lie in bed thinking about the lapse of time. How could you lose track of six hours while you were out on Hawk Mountain? Could Jeb be right? Could it really have something to do with aliens? You're curious to go back up to the mountain again. If you look carefully, maybe you'll find a clue.

The next day at the ranch is your last. You're so busy working, you hardly have time to think about what happened to you yesterday.

In the evening, after everyone's gone to bed, you hear a whimpering outside your door.

Turn to page 50.

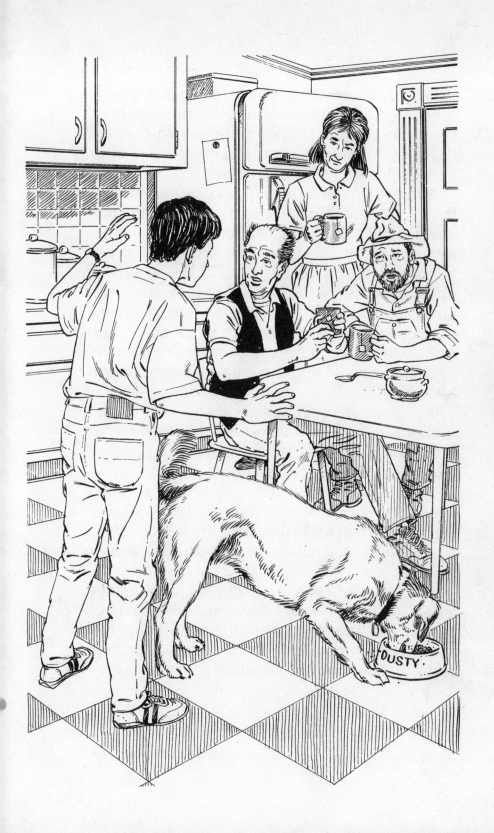

When you arrive home that evening, you don't even mention to your family about what happened to you on Hawk Mountain. No one will believe you, anyway, you realize. Either that or they'll think you've gone daffy.

During the months ahead you give less and less thought to your experiences up there—until one day the following spring when you catch an interesting show on TV. A man is interviewing several people who claim to have seen UFOs. A couple of photographs are shown, and after each one, a scientist named Dr. Gruen comes on to explain how the photograph was just a trick or an optical illusion. After watching this program for a while, you're convinced that aliens haven't visited Earth after all.

The program starts to get pretty boring, and you're about to turn it off when a little gray-haired lady comes on. She seems so earnest that you decide to listen awhile longer.

"My name is Hattie Clemens," she says, "and I live in Eureka Springs, Arkansas. I didn't see a UFO, and I didn't take a picture, but I'm sure that I had an alien encounter. One afternoon I took a walk in the woods. After a while I needed a rest, so I sat down near a spring coming out from under a rock. Next thing I knew, I started to feel dizzy. Then suddenly it was dark outside. Several hours had just passed, and I just don't know where they went! I know I didn't fall asleep."

Turn to page 47.

At first you're so fascinated, you forget that you should be frightened. A wave of panic sweeps over you. You want to get out!

You turn and start back in the direction you came from. Somehow it seems farther than you would have expected. In fact, there seems to be an almost endless distance to the end of the light in every direction you turn.

You dart, first one way, then another. In a minute or two you realize that no matter which direction you go, no matter how fast you go, you don't get anywhere! You're trapped!

Turn to page 26.

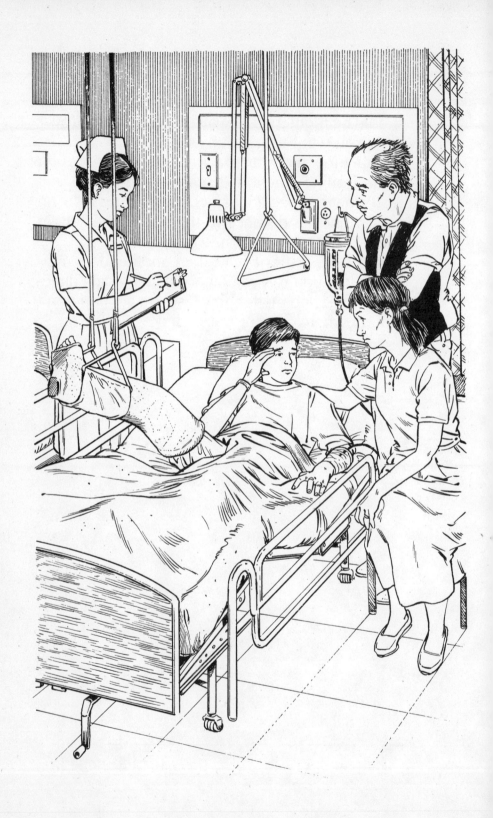

The next time you wake up, you're in a hospital bed. Your leg is in a cast, supported in a sling suspended from the ceiling. An IV tube is attached to your arm. Your uncle Howard and aunt Nan are sitting by your bedside, and a nurse is standing nearby.

"Welcome back," Uncle Howard says. "You sure had us scared. For a while there we weren't sure if you'd make it."

"The doctor says your leg should be all right," Aunt Nan says. "You'll be walking on it again in three or four weeks."

You try to smile. "Thanks for everything," you manage to say. "I'm sorry I put you to so much trouble."

"Don't worry about it," Uncle Howard says. "We're just glad you're okay."

"The one you should thank is Dusty," Aunt Nan says. "He woke us up at two in the morning and wouldn't stop barking till we realized you were missing. He's the one that led the rescue team to Hawk Mountain."

The End

16

You turn out the light and lie in bed, thinking about Hattie Clemens and what happened to her in Eureka Springs, Arkansas. Her experience was very similar to yours: a walk in the woods, a rest by a spring, then memory loss. Hearing about it makes you all the more eager to follow up on your discovery.

Uncle Howard and Aunt Nan have invited you back to their ranch again for a couple of weeks next summer, on the condition that you promise not to go up on the mountain at night. Even with that restriction, you're sure you could learn something new up on Hawk Mountain. One thing you'd like to do is dig down in the area where you saw the ground open up. You just might find some clues there.

You're about to write your aunt and uncle that you accept their invitation, when you happen to see an article in the newspaper about a certain Professor Burns of the Institute for UFO Research at the University of Colorado. The article says that the professor is setting up an expedition to investigate reports concerning a group of picnickers who blacked out for several hours while hiking in Steamboat Springs, a hundred miles or so to the west. He's looking for volunteers.

Turn to page 59.

"Do not be afraid," the creature says. "We are Cretians. We mean you no harm."

You remove the mug from the flaps on the end of the Cretian's outstretched trunk. "Where am I?" you ask. "And how do you know our language?"

"You are on the planet Balya," the creature answers. "We have learned your language while seeding your planet. You have been brought here for us to study."

The foul air is beginning to get to you. Your throat feels raw, and you start to cough and wheeze. You bend over, putting the bowl and the mug on the floor, afraid you're going to pass out. At that moment one of the Cretians races toward you, holding a cylindrical tank in its trunk. It turns the nozzle on the tank toward you, and a dense, smoky cloud envelops your head. You slump to the floor, gasping for air.

You hear the Cretians talking in a strange language. They seem to be arguing. The one with the tank moves back.

You look up at the two Cretians who brought you the food and drink. "I need fresh air," you plead.

One of them steps closer, staring at you with its great, bulging eyes. "That was fresh air," he says in a kindly voice, "but it doesn't seem to be helping you."

Your eyes are watering from the smog; tears are streaming down your cheeks. "What is this place?" you say. "And why did you come to Earth?"

Turn to page 62.

18

Having decided to leave Dusty behind, you get increasingly nervous as you set off for the mountain trail. You begin to wish you'd taken him along. As you climb the mountain, you have a feeling you're taking one chance too many coming up here again.

Something keeps driving you on. Maybe it's the spirit of adventure that motivated the famous explorers of history. Maybe it's just that you're stupid.

When you reach the ledge below Table Rock, you hug the wall of the cliff, careful not to take any false steps. You're halfway along the ledge when the moon disappears behind a cloud. Suddenly it's pitch-dark. You stand frozen, afraid of slipping and plunging over the side.

You wait for the moon to come out, but the sky grows even darker. The wind picks up. A storm seems to be coming in your direction.

You realize you can't stand on the ledge all night. You have to start heading back. Carefully you take a step; then another. Your foot comes down on a loose rock, and suddenly your legs are sliding out from under you! You clutch for a handhold, but you're sliding helplessly, bouncing down the steep rock face, banging your body into projecting rocks. Just as you think you're a goner, a small tree growing out of a lower ledge stops you. The force whips your body around it, and you feel a stabbing pain in your right leg as you lie there in a heap.

Turn to page 45.

"I was wondering," you say. "Perhaps the power dome could be a colony that aliens set up. Each power dome might be a home base for a separate community, if that makes any sense."

"That's a good guess," Dr. Vivaldi says. "Each power dome may be like a fish hatchery, providing nourishment for the eggs they've deposited there."

"You mean eggs out of which the aliens might hatch?" Derek asks.

"Exactly," the doctor replies. "But until we have more facts, these are only guesses."

The conversation ends for a while as the four of you eat your pizza. Professor Burns takes care of the check, and as you head out the door, he says, "Get to bed early tonight, everyone. We'll be leaving for Steamboat Springs first thing in the morning."

Turn to page 28.

You decide not to risk running outside. You watch helplessly as the Cretians seal off the breach. The fresh air that came through is now cut off, and foul air enters your lungs with each breath you take. It seems worse than ever after your having sampled the clean air from outside. Your throat and lungs feel raw and gritty. Your eyes are parched and sore.

A Cretian is sprawled out near the newly sealed gap. Several other Cretians are hovering over him, blowing thick smoke at him!

Suddenly you realize what's going on. The Cretians are administering first aid. The one lying on the floor must have been knocked out by the fresh air that came in through the breach! Now you know why they live in this polluted enclosure. Somehow, perhaps through some mutation, these creatures have developed so that they thrive on pollution. It's the fresh, oxygen-rich air that is deadly to them!

Turn to page 65.

22

You decide to visit your aunt and uncle, hoping to find some clues up at Table Rock. The moment you arrive at the ranch, your aunt Nan reminds you of your promise to stay away from the mountain at night. You assure her that you will, and you mean it. After all, it was generous of them to invite you back again after all the worry you caused them last summer.

For the first week you're so busy you have no chance during the day to hike up the mountain. The first free day you have after helping your uncle Howard repair fences is a rainy Sunday. A couple of ranch hands invite you to ride into town with them to see a movie, but you turn them down. You've been waiting a year to go back to the mountain, and now that you have the chance you're not going to let it pass.

Your aunt Nan watches you as you get ready. "I'm not sure it's such a good idea for you to be going up there," she says. "That narrow ledge could be very slippery in the rain."

Go on to the next page.

"I'll be careful," you say. "And I'm taking Dusty along. If I'm late, it means something happened to the time, which I have no control over."

Aunt Nan smiles at you. "I don't think that will happen," she says. "Quite a few local people took an interest in your story after Jeb spread it around. There have been several expeditions up to Table Rock in the year you've been away, and no one experienced a loss of time or saw anything unusual."

"Well," you say, "maybe I'll have better luck." You borrow a spade from Jeb, whistle for Dusty to follow, and start up the mountain.

Turn to page 60.

With map in hand, Professor Burns leads you to a place where the stream broadens into a good-sized pond. "See those bubbles rising in the middle?" he says. "That's where the warm springs are coming up."

Turning to you, he continues, "Why don't you stay with Dr. Vivaldi and explore this end; Derek and I will go up toward the other end. We'll be out of sight of one another, but we'll still be within shouting distance. My guess is that if we wait long enough, we'll see something interesting."

You and Dr. Vivaldi sit on a fallen log, where you begin your vigil. After an hour, Dr. Vivaldi walks toward the other end of the pond to check on the others. Minutes later you see something rising out of the grassy glade near the edge of the pond—it's the power dome!

The dome is about the size and shape of an igloo, but it's certainly not made of ice; it seems to be composed of a glowing, rose-tinted light. You can't seem to take your eyes off it!

Turn to page 9.

26

The reality of what has happened strikes you. Dejected, you remove your helmet and slump to the floor, surprised to find that it is yet another dense plane of light.

You close your eyes, hoping that you're dreaming, even though you know that you're not. Whoever controls the power dome has technology far more advanced than anything on Earth. All you can do now is hope that they are friendly.

Suddenly you sense that you are moving, that the power dome is taking you somewhere! You can only imagine that when the others come looking for you, they will find no trace of you.

Of course, they will report your disappearance to the police and to your family, but if the police send scuba divers into the pond, thinking that you may have drowned, they won't find anything. Only Professor Burns, Dr. Vivaldi, and Derek will know that you must be inside the power dome, perhaps on Earth; or perhaps you're in another dimension, or on another planet, a very long way away.

You fight back the tears, wondering what will happen to you and whether you will ever see your friends and family again.

Turn to page 52.

You run up to greet the humans. The young man, it turns out, is Arturo Vivaldi, the grandson of the famous scientist, Dr. Nera Vivaldi! You suddenly realize how long you've been living on this planet. Arturo wasn't even born yet when you left Earth!

He tells you that he and his wife, Maria, left Earth several years ago in search of a planet upon which humans could seek refuge.

"What do you mean?" you ask.

"Things couldn't be worse, I'm afraid," Arturo answers. "Earth has become hopelessly polluted, and the temperature has increased tremendously. The sea level has risen so much that the coastal regions have been covered with water.

"The planet has been taken over by these insectlike creatures who seem to thrive on the pollution. Not many humans are left. Unless we can find another home, they too will die.

"Our astronomers located this planet as our only hope, and Maria and I were sent to investigate it. We landed last night and have found it to be as beautiful as Earth must have once been. We have already radioed a message back home, letting the remaining earthlings know it's safe to come here."

Turn to page 85.

The next morning you have a quick breakfast together and hit the road just a little after seven. Professor Burns drives the jeep, and Dr. Vivaldi sits next to him. You and Derek take the backseats.

The city of Boulder is nestled against the eastern slopes of the Rockies. You're hardly out of town when the car starts climbing. You swallow a couple of times as the altitude increases, trying to ease the pressure in your ears. Soon you're in a different world—one with snow-capped, fourteen-thousand-foot peaks in almost every direction.

Turn to page 4.

Dusty comes over and sniffs at your discovery. Suddenly he starts to bark sharply, then he backs off and looks at you, perfectly still and quiet.

"We've found some kind of clue, Dusty," you say. "Now we've got to figure out what it is."

You probe around the hole a little with your spade to see if there are any other clues, but you don't turn up anything else. You fill up the hole as best you can, stuff the capsule into your backpack, and start down the mountain. Dusty runs on ahead.

When you get back to the ranch, it's about two in the afternoon. There's a note for you on the kitchen table. Everyone's gone into town to the movies, it says.

You take a hot shower and change into dry clothes. Then you put the capsule on the kitchen table and study it.

Turn to page 36.

You look into the opening you've cut in the capsule. The inside is just more of the same foul-smelling oil and sludge. But then you notice something else there—a creature about the size of a small rabbit. It looks, more than anything else, like an insect larva. It has six appendages that, as yet, are only half-formed. Four of them look like legs, the front two are more like trunks, or antennae. The creature has a head that seems too large for its body, and its mouth takes up the whole lower half of its face. The upper half consists of two large, bulging eyes.

The creature stirs. It's alive!

Turn to page 48.

You've hardly reached the berries when you hear a noise in the bushes ahead. You stop short and peer through the foliage cautiously.

Several shapes are visible. They look like humans, except they're covered with long, shaggy hair, much like apes. They look to be no more than four feet high. These hominoids move gracefully through the bushes, plucking berries and dropping them into bags made out of cloth.

Watching them makes you realize just how hungry you are. You pull off the nearest berry and pop it into your mouth. It's delicious. You start to pick some more when two of the shaggy creatures start toward you.

At first you're afraid they are going to attack; then you see that they are offering you some berries to eat. They start talking to you in their own peculiar language, one of clicks and whistles and other sounds unheard of in human speech.

You take the berries and thank them for their kindness, although you can't imagine they can understand a word of what you say. They are being friendly, however, so it hardly matters.

Unlike the Cretians, these creatures don't seem advanced enough to have traveled through space. You doubt if they've ever heard Earth languages. You can't expect them to learn yours, so you'll have to learn theirs. It may be your only hope of survival.

Turn to page 78.

Apparently your intentions weren't good enough. Within a couple of days Slimy is dead. It never touched anything you gave it, instead it got more and more listless until it no longer moved at all. Sadly you bury the little alien in a grove of spruce trees behind the barn.

Before your vacation ends, you make one more trip to Table Rock Spring, but nothing unusual happens.

When you return home, you write a letter to Professor Burns and tell him all about Slimy and your experiences. You ask if he made any discoveries at Steamboat Springs, and if there's anything you can do to help.

A few weeks later you receive a letter in reply. It comes not from Professor Burns, but from his sister, Mrs. Kraft, who writes to you as follows:

"I am writing in response to your letter addressed to my brother, Hendrick. Several weeks ago, while investigating a site in Steamboat Springs, Colorado, he mysteriously disappeared. No one knows what happened to him or where he went. There are no clues. If he ever returns, I will give him your letter."

Professor Burns never does turn up, and you never hear from him or his sister again. Instead you are left with a lot of questions: Why was the creature you discovered left on Earth? Why did it die so quickly? And what happened to Professor Burns?

The End

34

You tell the Balyans that it is time for you to try and return to Earth. Although they are sad to see you go, they understand. They summon friends from many of the neighboring caves and throw you a farewell party.

You leave early the next morning, walking through the forest, around the green lake, and across the meadows until you reach the same enclosure from which you escaped.

There are no visible openings. You walk around the perimeter, looking for anything resembling a door or a window.

The size of the structure is staggering. Its circumference must be well over a mile. The gray, plastic-like surface seems perfectly smooth.

After walking about halfway around the structure, you see something unusual—a slim section of the wall that seems to be made of pure light. Your guess is that it's a wall like the wall of the power dome back on Earth. It seals the air in tightly, yet humans and Cretians can pass through it with ease.

Turn to page 42.

36

You tap it with a spoon; it doesn't sound hollow. You run a kitchen knife over its surface. The material is hard, but you're able to scratch it. You might be able to saw it with a hacksaw. That seems like the only way to open it and see what's inside.

You get a hacksaw from the toolshed and take the capsule out to the workroom in the barn. You're about to get started when you begin to have second thoughts. Maybe you should ask someone for advice. Perhaps Professor Burns from the Institute for UFO Research can help you.

If you decide to saw the capsule open,
turn to page 84.

If you decide to call Professor Burns for advice,
turn to page 110.

"This was no ordinary star," Hrk continues. "It flashed across the sky like a great meteor and landed near the sea of the white waves. Instead of finding a pitted rock from space, our people found a ship, and creatures no one had ever seen before. They built the large enclosures like the one you came from.

"When they were finished, our people never saw them again. They remained inside their walls. In turn, we Balyans never go near these enclosures, for it is told in many legends that a foul wind may blow from them and destroy us."

You listen to this story with great interest. "Tell me, Hrk," you say, "many nights I have looked up at the sky. I have seen all the stars and the two blue moons, but I have never seen Cretia, the brown planet you have mentioned."

The Balyan nods. "Cretia is no more," he says. "It was destroyed by a star."

"When did this happen?"

"A few moons before the creatures came to the land of the Balyans."

You nod. "I think I understand what happened," you say. "The creatures that live within the enclosures call themselves Cretians. They must have come from the planet Cretia.

"At some time in their history, their planet must have become increasingly polluted. Over time, they were able to adapt to these conditions, evolving so that eventually they *needed* pollution in order to survive."

Turn to page 73.

38

It seems as if the best thing to do is to leave the creature in the capsule as it is. If it really is from outer space, its needs may be different from those of human babies or animals. The slimy goo in the shell may provide it with nutrients it needs to develop and survive.

You take a closer look at the strange little creature. It sure is disgusting looking. I think I'll call it Slimy, you say to yourself.

Rather than run the risk of losing your discovery, you put the capsule in an unused wire mesh chicken coop in the barn outside the workroom. If Slimy manages to crawl out of the capsule, it won't get far.

Back at the ranch, everyone is fascinated by your discovery. No one knows what to do, but they all have different suggestions. One of the ranch hands wants to kill the creature. "You can't trust a thing like that," he warns. His suggestion is quickly rejected, and you decide to wait and see what happens.

Turn to page 49.

"Well, that's an intelligent creature," Uncle Howard says, "we know that much."

"It can't talk, and it's only a baby," Aunt Nan says, "but for all we know, it may be more intelligent than we are."

"But we can't keep it around here," Uncle Howard says. "We've got to call the authorities."

Aunt Nan rests a hand on your shoulder. "It's for the best," she says. "Besides, you'll be going home in a couple of days, and it's not possible for you to take Slimy with you. And we can't take care of it until next year when you come visit."

"Do you want to make the call, or shall I?" your uncle asks you. From his tone, you know you can't argue the point any further.

"I'll make the call," you say.

The question is, Whom should you call? Your first thought is to call Professor Burns. But then it occurs to you that if something happens after you leave, and it turns out that Slimy is dangerous, you might be held responsible. Maybe you should call the police and see what they advise.

If you decide to call Professor Burns, turn to page 88.

If you decide to call the police, turn to page 74.

You, Uncle Howard, and Aunt Nan look on with mixed curiosity and disgust.

"I can't stand to look at this any longer," Aunt Nan says. She tugs at your uncle, and a minute later both of them say good-bye, leaving you and Professor Burns alone with the creature.

"Thank goodness I hit on the right formula the first time," the professor says. "I don't think there's any danger Slimy will starve now. The fact that it has a good appetite and moves easily tells me that it's healthy enough to travel. I'm going to take it back to the lab at the university for further study. We'll have some of the top scientists in the country examine it. I want to thank you for all of your help."

"I wish I could visit your lab and talk to some of those scientists," you say.

"You're more than welcome," he says. "In fact, we could use you as part of our investigating team. You already know more about these aliens than we do. You're one of our experts!"

"I don't really have the money to travel to Boulder," you say. "Besides, I have to get home— school's starting soon."

"Don't worry about either of those things," Professor Burns says. "The University Research Fund will pay all your expenses. As for school, you'll learn more working on the project for a month than you would in class in a year."

Turn to page 90.

You walk right through the wall. You feel no resistance or pain, only the same tingling sensation that you experienced before. The light envelops you once again, and immediately you start to cough. You'd forgotten how polluted the air is inside the enclosure. After breathing fresh air from outside, it seems especially foul.

You start to panic! There's no way you can survive in this atmosphere. Then you see what you had hoped to find—a power dome. It's mounted on a huge dolly, glowing with light, just like the one back on Earth. Three robots are moving it toward the wall of light where you just entered. Perhaps they're going to launch it!

You have an urge to enter the power dome—this could be your chance to escape. The thing is, you have no idea where it will be sent. What if it goes to some horrible planet? You could be forced to spend your remaining days in agony! Still, there's a chance it's headed for Earth.

Maybe you should just approach the Cretians and ask them for help. Whatever your decision, you have to make it fast.

If you enter the power dome, turn to page 68.

If you ask for help, turn to page 80.

You call Professor Burns, accept his invitation, and arrive in Colorado on July 15. The professor meets you at the airport and drives you to the Boulderado Hotel, where you'll be staying overnight.

That evening, you join him and his son, Derek, who is a couple of years older than you. Professor Burns asks for a table for four; you look around to see who the other person will be. Just then, a middle-aged lady with deep brown eyes comes over. She looks rather familiar to you—in fact you remember having seen her on TV. She's Dr. Nera Vivaldi, the famous expert on interspecies communication.

After Professor Burns introduces you to Dr. Vivaldi, the four of you order pizza and beverages. Dr. Vivaldi then tells you that she agrees with your theory about the loss of memory that you suffered having something to do with aliens from outer space.

"But what I can't understand is why aliens would make people lose their memories," you say.

The doctor casts a look toward Professor Burns. "To keep humans from discovering their presence, wouldn't you agree, Professor?"

"Or, to put it another way," he says, "to keep humans from remembering that they've seen them."

Turn to page 57.

44

It's fresh air—as good as any on Earth! The air is coming through the breach in the wall. You walk toward it, taking it into your lungs. Instantly you feel better. If only you can get through to the other side!

"Stand back from the breach!" a Cretian shouts. "You will be killed; the air is deadly."

You have no time to think. In a few seconds they will have sealed off the breach. Your instinct tells you to run, but perhaps you shouldn't risk it. However, if you don't get fresh air soon, you may die.

If you try to run through the breach in the wall, turn to page 70.

If you decide not to risk it, turn to page 21.

The moon is still hidden, and the night sky surrounds you. From where you are you can't even tell how far you've fallen. You feel your leg with your hand. The slightest touch hurts. You're sure it's broken. As you lie there in pain, you realize you are in deep trouble.

You start to yell for help, but you know it won't do you any good; there's no one around for miles. Your aunt and uncle won't miss you until after sunup. By the time they find you, who knows what will have happened to you? You try not to think about it, but the pain is unbearable. Your head starts to spin. You lose consciousness.

Slowly you come to. It takes a few moments for you to remember what happened to you and where you are. It's still pitch-dark out; you have no idea what time it is. At least you're still alive—so far.

You hear the sound of barking, but you're not sure if you're imagining it. You look toward the direction of the sound. Then you hear it again. It's Dusty, you realize. He must have known you'd return to the mountain and followed your scent. You try to call to him, but you're weak. The pain is unbearable. Moments later you pass out once again.

Turn to page 15.

"Well," says the interviewer, "if you didn't fall asleep, how do you account for what happened to you?"

"I can't be sure," the woman answers, "but it is my belief that aliens were nearby. For some reason they wanted me to forget whatever I saw. Something happened to me during those missing hours, I'm sure of it. I just can't recall what."

"Thank you, Ms. Clemens," the interviewer says as the camera switches to the scientist. "How do you account for this story, Dr. Gruen?"

The scientist strokes his close-clipped beard a moment. "Well," he says, "there are many possible explanations: Ms. Clemens may have fainted. Or she might have had a small stroke, and then recovered after a few hours' rest. Her story is really no different from any of the other stories we have examined here tonight. There must be a logical explanation.

"Just because something unusual happens, it doesn't mean UFOs caused it. After all our research and investigations, there is still no proof that aliens have been visiting our planet."

"Thank you for being with us, Dr. Gruen," the interviewer says. "Join us next week when we'll be—" At that moment you click the TV off.

Turn to page 16.

48

You stand back, hypnotized, as you realize that you're looking at some kind of alien life-form. It certainly doesn't look dangerous—it's just a baby, unable to do anything but wiggle around in its slimy capsule. You wonder what it will grow up to be. From the looks of it, it may be something horrible; but then again, maybe not. After all, caterpillars turn into butterflies.

You've just exposed this creature to a strange environment, and you have no idea how to care for it. It's unlikely that anyone else will know how either, or that it will live much longer.

The creature is still wiggling around in its shell. You wonder whether you should open the capsule up and take it out. You may be able to take care of it better that way. On the other hand, maybe it would be wiser to leave it as it is until you figure out what to do.

If you take the creature out, turn to page 72.

If you leave it in the capsule, turn to page 38.

In the meantime you visit Slimy every day. As the days go by it grows, and most of the smelly, oily goo in the capsule disappears. The creature must be eating that horrible stuff, you realize. The only thing is, it's almost all gone. You've got to figure out how to get more before the supply runs out.

After some experimentation, you mix a bucketful of used motor oil, garbage, bits of plastic, and some battery acid. It looks and smells a lot like the goo Slimy's been eating.

You put it next to the cage, and by the next day Slimy has managed to split open the capsule and actually eaten some of it.

Turn to page 76.

50

You open the door, and Dusty jumps on you, wanting to play.

The rest of the house is dark. Your aunt and uncle have gone to bed. You walk through the dining room onto the deck outside.

The weather is calm and clear—a little chilly but not really that cold. The moon is high in the night sky. Dusty is jumping up and down with excitement. He thinks you're going to take him out for a hike. You wonder if he has the same hunch that you have—that you should return to Table Rock tonight.

In the bright moonlight, you should have no trouble finding your way up the mountain. You have plenty of time to go and still get back by dawn. With any luck, your aunt and uncle will never know you left.

You put some cookies, an orange, and a canteen of water in your backpack and strap it on. Dusty is jumping around like crazy. As you walk across the back deck, you almost trip over him.

Maybe you should leave Dusty at the ranch. If he starts barking, he might spoil your chances of seeing any aliens. On the other hand, you would feel safer having him along.

If you decide to leave Dusty, turn to page 18.

If you decide to take him along, turn to page 8.

After four hours of driving, you cross Rabbit Ears Pass and begin your descent into an expansive valley. The mountain on the east side of the valley is etched with ski runs. Beneath them are several villages, where skiers stay while they're enjoying the slopes.

Professor Burns passes the town and turns off onto an old logging road. There are several forks in the road, and a couple of times he stops to consult his map. After driving a few miles farther, he pulls to a stop at an eroded, gravelly area near a narrow stream. The four of you put on your helmets as you get out of the jeep.

Turn to page 24.

52

Much time has passed, but how much you can't tell. The air has turned foul, as if there were a diesel engine nearby, making smelly smoke. It gives you a headache.

You find yourself lying on some kind of soft plastic shelf that is raised up off the floor. The space around you is still endless. Although it is well lit, soon you can't see because of the smog!

You have no idea where you are—whether you're on Earth, in space, or on some other distant planet. The fact is, you hardly care. All you care about now is getting out of this place.

You stiffly raise yourself up. Just then, two insectlike creatures come toward you. Their heads are grasshopperlike, with great bulging eyes. Each of them is about four feet long and has four legs. The creatures have two more appendages that look like small-sized elephant trunks.

Instinctively you jump back; the creatures stop. A third one enters, holding a bowl with one of its trunks. It seems to be offering you food. You smile at them and take the bowl, which is filled with what looks like tiny, oily biscuits. Another creature approaches, this one offering you a mug filled with brown liquid. To your astonishment the creature speaks to you in your own language.

Turn to page 17.

54

Dusty is barking loudly. You start to feel dizzy. The next thing you know, you're blinking your eyes in the bright sunlight. You can't believe it! It's now midmorning, even though it was the middle of the night just seconds ago. You know you didn't fall asleep, you're still standing where you were. But what happened?

You examine the ground, but it looks exactly as it did the day before. There's no sign of any hole where it seemed to split open. You scratch your head, trying to figure out what went on last night. Where did the time go?

"Well, Dusty," you say. "I'd like to stick around and investigate, but we've got to get back to the ranch. They're bound to have missed us by now."

You hurry back down the mountain as fast as you can.

Your aunt and uncle are waiting on the ranch house deck for you when you return. Uncle Howard stands up when he sees you coming. "Don't you ever learn? You've turned into a real nuisance, going up to the mountain at night. It's a wonder you didn't fall off that cliff."

Go on to the next page.

"Really," your aunt Nan says, "if you want to visit us again next summer, you'll have to promise not to do this again."

You start to explain, but your uncle cuts you off. "It's almost noon," he says. "We've got to leave to take you to the airport in twenty minutes."

"Gosh, I'd almost forgotten. I'm going home today," you say.

"I hope your memory improves before school starts again," your aunt says, shaking her head.

Turn to page 12.

Your pizza arrives, and you slide a big slice onto your plate.

"I didn't want to tell you this over the phone," Professor Burns says. "Before the picnickers at Steamboat Springs lost their memories, one of them managed to take this color snapshot."

He lays the photo on the table for you to examine. It shows a dome-shaped structure about eight feet high. It's glowing with a rose-tinted green light and appears to be giving off energy.

"I believe it's a power source that the aliens use while they're exploring the earth. For that reason I call it a power dome," he says.

"It could serve as an information-gathering module," says Dr. Vivaldi, "though if that were the case, I would think there would be an antenna on it."

"That is, unless their technology is so advanced that they don't need one," Derek says.

"That's quite possible," Dr. Vivaldi says. "The tendency is to think that alien technology will be similar to ours, only more advanced. But we should keep in mind that they may operate from a totally different set of rules than we do, ones we can't even begin to imagine."

Turn to page 20.

58

You move your hand closer and closer to the dome, until your fingers are almost touching it. Then, with your heart in your mouth, you pass your hand swiftly through the light.

Surprisingly, you feel no temperature change or pain; only a strong tingling sensation as your hand disappears through the wall.

You quickly pull back your hand and anxiously examine it. It seems fine, no different than if you had passed it through a shaft of sunlight. Your curiosity is even greater now. With one swift motion you pass your whole arm through the light. Then, anxious to see what's inside, you walk through the wall!

As you pass through, your whole body tingles. Once inside, however, you feel as normal as ever. Blinking your eyes, you try to make sense out of what you see—the area seems huge, much larger than it appeared from the outside. You can see no clearly defined shapes or shadows, only light. It seems to form all around you, supporting you so that you feel almost weightless. Although you can see quite far, you also feel enclosed, as if the light is restricting you, holding you in place.

You take a few steps forward, reaching out with your hands, thinking you might find mirrors that are creating the illusion of depth. But there are no mirrors, only light.

This is no ordinary light, you realize. It's like nothing you've seen on Earth—it's a form of light; but it is also matter.

Turn to page 13.

You telephone Professor Burns and tell him about your experience at Table Rock Spring in California. He's very interested in your story and asks if you'd like to join him on the expedition to Steamboat Springs that he's planning in July.

You ask your parents if you can join Professor Burns's research team. They tell you that you can either go on that trip or visit your uncle Howard and aunt Nan again, but you can't do both.

If you visit your aunt and uncle, you can investigate Table Rock and look for clues. If you join the professor and go to Steamboat Springs, who knows what you'll find. Either vacation promises to be exciting.

If you decide to go with the team to Steamboat Springs, turn to page 43.

If you decide to visit your aunt and uncle again, turn to page 22.

60

The rain slows you down quite a bit. By the time you reach Table Rock Spring, you're pretty tired. It's kind of a letdown to finally get there—the place seems so deserted and lonely. You start to look around when Dusty begins to make funny noises. He starts toward the trail as if he wants you to go back. For a second you think it's because he senses danger, but then you realize he just wants to get out of the rain.

You take your spade over to the place where you saw the ground split open. The ground is soft and wet, and you're able to dig easily and quickly. You take a close look at each spadeful of dirt before heaving it to the side, hoping to find a clue.

After digging down a couple of feet, you hit a rock. As you dig around it, you begin to feel excited. It's too smooth to be a rock, you realize; its shape is too regular. It's gray in color, about the size and shape of a football, and seems to be made of metal or some kind of ceramic—definitely a capsule of some kind, quite possibly an egg!

After a few minutes you're able to dig it out of the ground. You were afraid it would be too heavy, but it's light enough for you to carry. You examine it, looking for a seam or an opening, but it seems perfectly smooth. You shake it, but it makes no noise. What is this thing?

Turn to page 29.

62

One of the Cretians moves in closer. "The outside air is bad on our planet," he says. "We are forced to live in enclosures such as the one we're in now. Earth will one day be like this enclosure, too. It will be much better for us to live there. That is why we're planting our seeds there. As soon as Earth is ready, we will populate your planet."

"What do you mean, when Earth is ready?" you ask.

"As soon as the impurities are gone from your planet. When conditions are suitable."

You still have more questions, but it's hard to think straight. The polluted air is making you ill.

You're struggling to think about what you can do when an alarm sounds. Through the haze you see dozens of Cretians running in all directions. Some of them are carrying scaffolding and wooden planks; others have tools of various kinds.

The one nearest you shouts over the noise. "There's a breach in the wall," he says. "We must help mend it." In a second he lopes off. Slowly you stumble after him.

Through the smog you come upon the curving wall of the building. It is pitted and scarred, apparently eaten away by toxic fumes. In one place it has worn completely through. As you stare at the Cretians running to patch the gap, a gust of air comes through it and hits your face.

Turn to page 44.

One by one other Cretians come up and greet you warmly. They feel very friendly toward anyone from Earth, they tell you, and let you know that your planet is almost ready for colonization!

You try to imagine what this news will mean to those back home, but you can't think straight—your head is spinning, your throat feels like it's on fire, and your whole body hurts.

The Cretians realize you're sick and rush to help. One of them holds a cup to your lips. It's filled with the healthiest drink they know—toxic waste water. Your last meal turns out to be only a sip.

The End

In a moment the Cretian gets back on his feet. The smoke helped revive him, but the polluted air is making you dizzy. Your eyes are blurring, your head aching. You have the symptoms of carbon monoxide poisoning. This is an emergency. You've got to get fresh air!

You start toward the sealed breach, hoping that the Cretians will take pity on you and let you through. But before you can take another step, you stumble and fall.

A Cretian rushes over to you. He gently lifts your head with one of his trunks. He's trying to comfort you. Through blurry eyes, you see the others coming toward you, carrying the same hose they used to revive the fallen Cretian. They hold it gently above your face as thick smoke pours out.

You close your eyes and hold your breath, but you can't hold it for long. What was a lifesaving gas for the fallen Cretian is a toxic one for you. Your end comes slowly, and the last breath you take really is your last.

The End

You follow an overgrown trail through a grove of royal palms and orange-hued gumbo-limbo trees. Wild coffee plants, ferns, and orchids grow on either side of your path.

Professor Burns has just taken Slimy out of his case and put him on a leash when a blur of rose-tinted light rises from the ground ahead of you. It continues to rise in a graceful arc, then disappears into the clouds!

"That was the power dome!" Derek shouts.

"We have our work to do," Professor Burns says. "Let's go!"

The rest of you follow him as he hurries forward.

"Look," he calls, "the grass is still bent from the wind that was stirred up when the power dome took off."

"But not a single blade is charred," Dr. Vivaldi says. "The dome is obviously powered by something other than fuel."

"That's not surprising," the professor says.

"Look," you say, "Slimy is sniffing the ground where the power dome took off."

Go on to the next page.

67

The four of you watch as the alien creature walks around the site. To your disappointment he returns to his cage moments later without so much as a sound.

"It's time to use those supplies you brought, Dr. Vivaldi," Professor Burns says.

As you help Dr. Vivaldi unpack the supplies, you're surprised to see cans of industrial waste and a small gasoline engine with a hose attached to it. "What are you going to do with that?" you ask.

Turn to page 101.

68

You decide to enter the power dome, passing through its wall of light just as you did back on Earth. You feel the same tingling sensations and the same disorientation that you had before. Moments later, you begin to sense motion, a slow acceleration that never stops, and you know that you're being transported through space.

Then comes sleep. Just how long it lasts you can't be sure. When you awaken, you are still inside the same arched walls of light, only now you sense that you are no longer in motion. The power dome must have landed.

To your amazement the dome suddenly seems to dissolve around you, and you find yourself standing on open ground. A yellowish-red sunlight is shining upon you. The air smells strongly of sulphur and smoke.

You've been deposited in the middle of a marsh, one that is littered with plastic waste and debris. You begin picking your way through the trash, heading for the high ground you can make out in the distance ahead.

Through the smog you can also make out the outline of a hill covered with dead trees. A dead sea gull lies in your path. At once it becomes painfully clear—it's unlikely that an identical creature would have evolved on another planet. You are back on Earth, at some period of time in the future!

Turn to page 89.

70

You rush toward the opening. One of the creatures lashes out, wrapping a trunk around your leg, tripping you.

You're able to wheel halfway around, unwrapping yourself from the Cretian's ropelike trunk. You land on your hands, then sprint through the breach, gathering more and more strength as the clean air fills your lungs. Glancing back, you discover that the Cretians have not followed you; they seem intent on sealing the wall, avoiding the oxygen.

Turn to page 81.

72

You decide to take the creature out in order to better care for it. You don't want to get any more of the smelly slime on you, so you wrap plastic around your gloves. Then you pick the creature up and take it to the sink, where you wash it gently in warm, soapy water.

Once cleaned up, it almost looks cute, the way a grasshopper does. Then you touch it for the first time with your bare fingers. Its scaly body feels smooth and soft. You need to give it a name, and you decide to call it Slimy.

Turn to page 6.

"They must have been aware of the terrible calamity that threatened their planet," you say. "The star that destroyed it was a comet, perhaps, or a stray meteorite. In order to escape, they fled to another planet. Yours was close by, so they came here. Once they landed, however, they must have found the air and the water to be much too fresh and pure for them. In order to survive, they were forced to build enclosures to contain their polluted atmosphere."

"But why did the Cretians bring *you* to this planet?" Hrk asks. "And will they ever let you return home?"

"Only the Cretians can answer those questions," you say. "And perhaps the time has come for me to ask them."

You understand a lot more about the Cretians now. The Balyans are highly intelligent, but their technology is primitive. From an earthling's standpoint, they are still living in the Stone Age. Only the Cretians can help you return home again.

You wonder if you should try to return to one of their enclosures. It's risky—they might think themselves under attack and kill you. And if they do let you inside, you won't be able to survive in their polluted air. Yet without their help, you may never return to Earth.

If you decide to try to enter the enclosure, turn to page 34.

If you decide to stay with the Balyans, turn to page 83.

74

You decide to phone the State Police. Your uncle Howard looks on as you make the call.

The officer who answers is far from sympathetic. "We can't tie up police phones listening to crank stories," he says, and hangs up.

Uncle Howard takes the phone from you and calls back. It turns out the police officer is an old fishing pal of his. The officer still doesn't believe your story, but he promises to send a squad car over sometime within the hour.

Turn to page 109.

"Then why did you say it's a great day for science?" Derek asks.

"Because instead of the pollution destroying us, we can use the aliens to help clean it up!"

"I see," you say. "It's perfect. We need them as much as they need us."

"Exactly," says Dr. Vivaldi. "It's called a *symbiotic* relationship, and there are many examples of it in nature. Take the cattle egret, for example. It rides around on the backs of cows and gets a free lunch by feeding off the flies that land there."

"Yes, symbiosis is a great system," Professor Burns says. "And now, for the first time it will work between the creatures of two different planets."

The End

From then on Slimy really starts to grow. Every day you go to the gas station in town to get more used motor oil and battery acid—it's the only thing Slimy will eat. Within a week it has grown to the size of a small dog.

One day, Dusty follows you into the barn. As soon as he sees Slimy, he starts to growl. You'd hate to think what would happen if Dusty got into that cage, so you put extra chicken wire over it and keep the door carefully bolted.

As the alien develops, your uncle Howard and aunt Nan look on with astonishment and concern.

One day they come with you to look in on the creature. To your amazement, Slimy has pried open a hole in the chicken wire, big enough to poke through one of its antenna-like trunks. The end of this appendage is curled around the bolt in the door of the cage, and Slimy is pulling it open!

Quickly you rush to the cage.

"Hold it shut," your uncle Howard calls. He runs over to the workbench and returns a moment later with a stout wooden plank, a hammer and some nails. In a few seconds he has the door nailed shut.

Slimy crouches in the back of the cage, its bulging eyes fixed on you.

Turn to page 39.

You slowly begin to learn their strange language of words, whistles, and clicks. Using sign language, they make you understand that you are welcome to live among them. Grateful, you move into one of their communal caves.

You find that they call themselves the Balyans, and refer to their planet as Balya. They live much the same way cavemen lived on Earth fifty thousand years ago, gathering food and hunting with spears and snares. They even make fire and cook. You watch as they pound out spearheads, bowls, and pans from metals they find in the rocks.

As time goes on, you play with the children on the swinging vines and go with the elders hunting for big game. You make friends with one of the young ones. His name can hardly be pronounced in English. The closest you can come to it is *Hrk*.

You live with Hrk and his family for many months, hunting, fishing, and even dancing with them at the festivals of their moons. Once you've learned their language well enough, Hrk is able to tell you much about life on their planet.

Go on to the next page.

One night, as the family sits around the campfire, he tells you of their history: "For as long as the grass has grown and the rivers have flowed, the Balyans have lived beneath the two blue moons, in the land of their ancestors," he says. "They have watched the sky and the brown planet known as Cretia as it moves among the stars.

"One day, many feasts ago, a new star appeared in the night sky, moving toward our home. In time it grew so bright, its light shone during the day."

Turn to page 37.

80

You decide not to take a chance on the power dome. You strain to see through the smog, hoping to find a Cretian who can help you.

You spot several of the weird, insectlike creatures; they're coming toward you, riding on a motorized cart. Puffs of yellowish smoke escape from its exhaust.

The Cretians hop down off the cart. At first you shrink back from their long, waving trunks; then you notice that they seem happy to see you.

"The human is back!" one shouts to the others, using your language. The others join in. "The human is back! The human is back!"

They pat you with their trunks and invite you onto their cart. You're glad to sit down—you were beginning to feel too sick to walk.

The Cretians take you to a chamber decorated with ornate lace sheets, like cobwebs in a musty barn. It looks like the last place where you'd want to spend any time.

Your eyes are itching, and you can't stop rubbing them. At the same time you're beginning to wheeze, as if you had a bad chest cold.

Turn to page 63.

The air smells as fresh and pure as a pine forest. You're free, but you have no idea what dangers lie in store for you. Though the air inside the enclosure was polluted, you were at least protected in there. For a second you think of going back. Then you realize you couldn't survive in that air for much longer.

You take a look all around you. A broad meadow with tall, fresh grass lies before you. Great rocks rear out of the land; they look like gray islands in a sea of green. Beyond the meadow, perhaps a mile from where you stand, lies a shimmering green lake. Wildflowers of every color bloom along its shores. The cliffs and hills in the distance are covered with stands of blue-needled pines. A sun, larger but not as bright as Earth's sun, hangs over the hills. It has a beautiful reddish tint, and you can look right at it without hurting your eyes.

Turn to page 96.

The years pass, and you live happily with the Balyans, making friends, hunting and fishing, and traveling across the vast, beautiful planet.

Every once in a while you hike back toward the enclosure you came from. You discover that it is just one of many such enclosures where the Cretians live, self-contained within their polluted, smelly environment.

Occasionally you see a light rising up into the sky, coming from one of these enclosures, and you wonder if the Cretians are migrating to Earth.

One evening, many years later, you see a glowing shape descending toward the ground. You lie awake most of the night, wondering what it was that you saw. Shortly before dawn the next morning some Balyans come and wake you.

"Come with us. There are creatures nearby—very much like you!" they say.

You jump up, splash your face with spring water, and follow the eager Balyans up the winding path. You come to a grassy place where a stream runs off a cliff, forms a pretty pool, and disappears into a cave.

You let out a whoop when you see the humans gathered in the grove. There's a young man and a young woman. They're dressed in space suits. A group of excited Balyans surrounds them.

Turn to page 27.

84

You decide to open the capsule by yourself. Carefully you set it in the big vise and begin to saw.

It's slow going. The capsule is made of harder material than you'd thought. After about ten minutes of hard work, you've only managed to cut a quarter of an inch into it.

For a moment you think you might as well give up. If the capsule turns out to be solid, you could end up sawing all day and have nothing to show for it but a sore arm. Your curiosity, however, is still strong, and you set to work again, harder than ever.

You've cut about a half inch into the capsule when a smelly, oily liquid begins to ooze out around the blade of your hacksaw. You're excited to have penetrated the shell, but what's coming out from the inside is unpleasant to say the least.

You keep sawing as the black, oily substance continues to leak out. Some of it gets on your hands, and some drips down onto the cement floor of the workroom. It smells awful. It's so disgusting, you go to wash your hands and put on work gloves.

You set some old newspapers underneath your work area to catch the dripping, oily liquid, then take the capsule out of the vise and put it on the newspapers. You carefully saw another slit perpendicular to the first one so you can remove a small section and see what's inside without splitting it in half.

Turn to page 31.

As Arturo explains all this, the Balyans wait patiently, unable to understand the strange language. Once you've explained to them who Arturo and Maria are, and why they have come, the Balyans welcome them.

You translate, telling Arturo and Maria that they will be as happy here as they were at home, or would be on any other planet in the galaxy.

"Think about it," Maria says. "The Cretians, who crave pollution, are all moving to Earth, and we humans, who need fresh air and water, are moving to this planet. It will be our new Earth!"

"It's wonderful," Arturo says. "We earthlings ruined our own planet, but we've been given a second chance."

You only hope that the planet Balya will remain as beautiful and peaceful as it is now.

The End

Reluctantly, you agree to let them examine the capsule. You stand back as the security man tries to cut into it. The shell is hard, and you look on helplessly as he jabs his knife straight in and splits it wide open.

To his surprise, as well as yours, foul-smelling slime and goo spill out, revealing an oil-stained creature about the size of a small rabbit. Two trunk-like appendages protrude from its ugly head. You shrink back from the sight of its scaly, oily body and the weird gaze of its bulging red eyes.

The security man is so startled that his hands fly out and strike the capsule. It goes sliding off the table and hits the hard floor, then breaks open. The little creature rolls out and crumples up in a slimy, lifeless heap.

"You idiot," you shout. "You killed it! It would have been of great scientific interest!"

"Calm down," the policeman says. "Judging by the looks of it, I think you can do without it."

Turn to page 107.

Professor Burns is tremendously excited when he hears from you. "Watch the creature day and night," he says, "and don't take the slightest risk—we can't let it escape. I'll take the first plane out that I can get. I should arrive at your uncle's ranch before noon tomorrow."

When you tell your uncle Howard and aunt Nan that Professor Burns is coming, they are annoyed at first that Slimy will be around for another night; but you're able to convince them that Professor Burns will know what to do better than the police would.

As promised, the professor arrives shortly before noon the next day. He's carrying an animal cage, a backpack, and a suitcase full of scientific equipment.

You take him over to the barn. For a long time he just stands there, staring at the alien creature.

"He's kind of gross," you explain, "so I've named him Slimy."

The professor takes a camera out and photographs the alien. Then he takes a canister out of his suitcase and unscrews the cap. A foul smell fills the air—a cross between rotten eggs and diesel fumes. He places the canister inside the cage he brought and pushes it up against the chicken coop where Slimy is housed. At the last second he opens the door, making a passageway between the two cages.

Slimy quickly scampers into the new cage. Within seconds he's lapping up the liquid in the foul-smelling canister.

Turn to page 41.

You start coughing and wheezing, just as you did in the Cretians' enclosure. You know you can't last long breathing this foul air. You head toward the top of the hill, hoping to find some sort of refuge.

As you reach the crest of the hill, you see a large, dome-shaped enclosure perched on the barren plain ahead. You sense at once what it is—a refuge that humans have built to protect themselves from the deadly pollution.

You feel sure you can reach it before you pass out and that the people there will take you in. The question is, what kind of life will await you?

The End

90

When they learn that you can get school credit for your scientific studies, your parents give you permission to spend the month of September at the University of Colorado, where Professor Burns has his lab.

After a week back at home, you arrive at the lab, eager to see how Slimy is doing. You take a limousine to the Boulderado Hotel, where you'll be staying. An hour later Professor Burns picks you up and drives you to the lab.

"The government is involved in this now," Burns says. "They are intensely interested in what this alien is like and how it came to Earth. NASA's sent over their top scientists, of course, and I even got a call from the president of the United States."

"While I was home, I heard some reports on TV," you say. "Most people think it's just another UFO story."

"That's just as well," Professor Burns says. "If the public knew what we've found out, they might panic. Nothing would scare people more than the thought of an alien invasion."

"Alien invasion!" you exclaim. "Is that what this is all about?"

The professor laughs. "Well, in a sense it is."

You reach the thick steel doors of the lab. "You'll be glad to know that Slimy seems quite content in the habitat we've created for him," Professor Burns says, waving his ID card at the guard and signing you in.

Turn to page 112.

"We have to assume the aliens reproduce much the same way that life does here on Earth," Professor Burns continues. "I wouldn't call it an invasion, but it's certainly a threat, and we need to find out exactly what we are dealing with here."

"Is there no way to spy on those places where the power domes have landed?" you ask. "Perhaps we could dig around in the area and see how many capsules they've planted."

The scientist nods. "Up till now, everyone who goes near these sites has experienced memory loss. Somehow the power domes are able to sense human presence and generate a highly focused electrical energy that wipes out short-term memory tracks. It's a problem we've never faced before on Earth, and we're working on a way to get around it."

After Professor Burns finishes talking, the two of you approach the glass enclosure. The alien sees you, flicks off the TV with the remote, and moves toward you. He presses against the glass, staring at you with his great bulging eyes.

"I think Slimy recognizes me," you say, waving at the creature. Surprisingly, he waves back with one of his trunks.

"You're right," Professor Burns says. "I think he's glad to see you."

Turn to page 102.

Two days later you, Professor Burns, and his
son, Derek, fly to Florida in a chartered jet. Slimy
sits next to you in a Plexiglas case, curled up in a
nest of rags soaked in used motor oil and battery
acid. As you approach the Miami airport, you look
down onto the vast sweep of grasslands.

"The Everglades is one of the most amazing
places in the world," Professor Burns says. "It's
actually a fifty-mile-wide river, six inches deep,
flowing southward toward Florida Bay. The ele-
vated areas, called hammocks, have some of the
most magnificent trees in the world—though
many of them have been felled by the great hur-
ricanes that sweep over southern Florida every
few decades. Others have been lost in prolonged
droughts.

"There's also an amazing abundance of wildlife
here: fantastic birds like pelicans, blue herons, and
flamingos, not to mention alligators, panthers, and
even manatees, animals that are as big as cows
and live almost entirely underwater."

"There can't be a more beautiful wilderness
area in America," you say.

"Indeed," Professor Burns replies. "However,
as time goes on it's been growing more and more
polluted from the runoffs of agriculture, industry,
and urban development. The Everglades have
also suffered in recent years from a number of
droughts and fires."

Go on to the next page.

Your plane hits some bumpy air pockets as it banks for its approach, but minutes later you're on the ground, eager to begin your investigation.

Turn to page 98.

"But if these aliens love pollution, why would they bury their capsules in beautiful wilderness areas such as the Everglades—why not in toxic-waste dumps or polluted harbors, and places like that?" Derek asks.

"That puzzled me, too," Professor Burns replies, "but I think I've come up with a theory. These eggs, or capsules, are like seeds that are planted in the fall and hatch in the spring. The aliens probably figured that if they revealed themselves too soon they might be destroyed. They didn't want to populate the earth until the planet was *ready*—until even the most beautiful, pure springs and wilderness areas were polluted.

"That's why these capsules were planted where they were. They were not set to open until pollutants trickled down to them. And at the rate our environment is deteriorating, that might not have been too far off!"

"Does this mean that there may be capsules planted in other areas around the world?" you ask.

"It's quite possible," the professor replies.

Turn to page 75.

Two days later you, Professor Burns, and his son, Derek, fly by chartered airplane to Eureka Springs, Arkansas. Slimy is kept in a sealed glass case in the backseat. Inside is a supply of canned carbon monoxide and a nest of rags soaked in used motor oil and battery acid.

As you come in for a landing, you look down at the scene below. There are no high mountains, just ridges, hills, and ravines, but the landscape is quite rugged nonetheless.

"These are the Ozarks," Professor Burns says. "There are some wonderful rivers and springs in the area, most of them still pure and unspoiled by man and pollution, although it will be a lot more developed I suppose within the next ten years."

That evening, you, Professor Burns, Derek, and Slimy camp on a ridge near the clear, bubbling spring where several picnickers were reported to have experienced memory loss. You sleep there overnight and wait all morning, taking turns walking Slimy on a leash, hoping that something will happen.

Turn to page 104.

96

Your spirits are lifted by this view, as beautiful as any you've seen. This must be what the earth would have looked like if there had been no industry or pollution. It makes you sad.

The chances of your finding food in this alien land may be slim. There's even a chance that some predator may leap forth and slay you. But you have no choice. Since you can't go back, you must go forward, across the meadow and toward the lake, where you hope to find food and drinkable water.

As you walk through the meadow, you watch for animals and insects that may be hiding in the knee-high grass. Several strange-looking butterflies flit across your path, and a flock of birds settles down on the lake. The planet seems to be very much like Earth.

When you reach a patch of wildflowers along the lake, you see many types of insects, including bees as big as small birds. You watch as they dart from flower to flower with amazing speed. They don't appear to have stingers, but you keep well clear of them just the same.

The water in the lake is crystal clear. You scoop some up in your hands and drink it. You're relieved—it's cool and refreshing.

Across the lake you see patches of blueberries. You set out at once to reach them. If they are edible, they'll provide you with much of the nutrition you'll need.

Turn to page 32.

98

You, Professor Burns, and Derek are met at the airport by Professor Burns's colleague, Dr. Nera Vivaldi, the famous expert on interspecies communication. She drives up in a van, which is so filled with equipment and supplies that there's hardly enough room for the four of you, especially after you've cleared away a place for Slimy.

Together you drive down Route One, then turn into Everglades National Park. Dark clouds are scooting across the sky. You hope the sun comes out before you get to your destination.

Special permission is required to leave the marked roads and trails, so you stop in at the Research Center and hook up with Sally Udell, a park ranger who has been assigned to accompany you on your expedition.

About ten minutes later you arrive at the Pine Glades parking area. Slimy's Plexiglas case fits snugly into Professor Burns's specially made backpack. You lock up the van, and with the rest of your supplies in your backpacks, you set off across the marsh, winding your way through the saw grass.

As you hike across the Everglades, you feel as if you're in the middle of the ocean. The flat grasslands stretch to the horizon in nearly all directions. But this sea of green is spotted with islands, studded with impressive stands of trees.

Sally has been guiding you toward one of these islands. Upon reaching it, you climb out of the swampy grass and find yourself standing on firm soil.

Turn to page 66.

You make a dash for the power dome, but before you reach its wall of light, a tremendous jolt surges through your body.

Sometime later, you wake up in a hospital. Two doctors and a nurse are standing by your bedside, alongside a man who looks vaguely familiar, though you can't remember who he is. In fact you can't remember anything!

One of the doctors is speaking in a very soft tone of voice. You strain your ears to hear what he is saying: "I'm afraid the patient's long-term memory has been destroyed."

"Derek and I experienced only a temporary memory loss," the other man says.

"Yes," the doctor responds, "but you said that the patient was standing only inches from the dome when the electrical waves were emitted."

"Still, the power dome must have sent out a much stronger signal than usual. They must have been protective of their baby—the creature we called Slimy."

"Whatever the reason," the doctor says, "I'm afraid your young friend will never remember anything again."

This doesn't worry you any, however. You've already forgotten what they were talking about.

The End

"We're going to pour dirty oil on the site and send carbon monoxide fumes down into the ground underneath it," Dr. Vivaldi replies in answer to your question.

"Is this all right?" you ask the ranger.

Sally nods. "It wouldn't be normally, but Professor Burns has special permission for this experiment from the Department of the Interior."

Her voice is drowned out by the shrill whine of the gasoline engine that Professor Burns has started up. You look on as Derek digs a little hole for the hose. In a minute carbon monoxide flows down into the soft, moist soil, almost surely killing insects and other tiny creatures in its path.

Slimy watches curiously for a moment, then leaves his cage and lopes over to the spot. He begins digging furiously, sending up dirt and fragments of roots with his two strong trunks.

"It's working!" Professor Burns says, grinning, as he pours more used crankcase oil into the hole.

"What's he doing?" Sally asks, but there's no need for anyone to answer. Small, ceramic-covered capsules are visible at the bottom of the hole. They are covered with an oily film that seems to be bubbling, as if it's being heated. A second later the capsules split open and little creatures just like Slimy crawl out.

Turn to page 106.

102

"I have an idea," you say. "Suppose we took Slimy back where I found him. Maybe the power dome would recognize him and not activate those electrical waves."

Professor Burns nods. "It's an interesting thought. I can't see any harm in trying." He gazes at the alien a few moments, then turns back to you. "Rather than return to the site in California near your uncle's ranch, I think we should follow up on these recent sitings in Arkansas and Florida. Either one is fine with me. I'll leave the choice up to you."

If you choose the site near Eureka Springs, Arkansas, turn to page 95.

If you choose the site in the Florida Everglades, turn to page 92.

You decide it would be safer to step back, rather than risk touching the strange, glowing dome. As you turn around, you suddenly start to feel dizzy. Then all you see is blackness except for the light of the stars. You look around for Dr. Vivaldi and the others, yelling their names, but there is no response.

By the dim light of the waning moon, you make your way back to Professor Burns's car. You're relieved to find it exactly where you left it; however, there's no sign of him, Derek, or Dr. Vivaldi.

You manage to catch some sleep in the back of the car until sunrise. In the morning you wander around, looking for your friends and calling their names, but without any luck. You walk back toward town, then report to the Steamboat Springs police what has happened and make arrangements for getting home.

Neither Dr. Vivaldi, Professor Burns, nor Derek are ever heard from again. To this day you're certain they were taken by aliens.

The End

104

A little before noon, just as a light drizzle begins to fall, a blur of light comes down from the sky and centers on the ground not 40 feet from your tent! The image forms into a dome of rose-tinted light. A small flock of birds, startled by the light, flies from some nearby trees. Beside you, Slimy strains at his leash.

You stare at the glowing dome. It seems to be resting on the ground, although for all you know, it might have rooted itself beneath the surface. Suddenly Slimy leaps forward, breaking his leash. A second later he passes through the surface of the dome as if he too were made of light!

"We've lost Slimy!" Derek cries.

"I'm afraid so," Professor Burns says, "and we can expect the dome to begin generating electrical waves. In a moment we may lose our memories. I suggest we back away from here in a hurry."

You want to rescue Slimy, even if it means entering the dome to do it. But should you risk it? Perhaps it would be best to observe the scene from your tent.

If you try to enter the power dome,
turn to page 99.

If you watch from your tent, turn to page 114.

106

"We can call the Special Forces team in now," Professor Burns says. "They will take these aliens to a special compound where we can monitor them."

Sally begins radioing back her report.

"What Special Forces team? What's happening?" Derek asks, as much in the dark as you are.

"I'll explain everything, don't worry. This is a great day for science," Professor Burns says, putting his arm around his son's shoulder. "Give me a couple of minutes. As soon as Sally is through with the radio, I need to use it. I promised to report the news directly to the president!"

On the way back to Miami, Professor Burns fills you in on what's happening. "This is all theory, of course," he says, "but it's our belief that these aliens might mean our salvation, although that's not their intention. They're not trying to take over the world, of that we are pretty sure. We don't know everything, but we can be reasonably certain of what's going on: the aliens need for survival what we need to get rid of—polluted air and water, waste and garbage!"

Turn to page 94.

By now people are starting to shout and complain because they haven't been allowed to pass. The security guard radios the maintenance crew to come and clean up the mess as the policeman turns back to service the other passengers.

"But you can't just throw it away," you say to the guard. "We need to preserve it for scientific study."

The guard looks over at the alien's tiny corpse and shakes his head. "You can't take that on the plane with you. It looks like it might spread a disease," he says. "The law is that dead animals have to be properly disposed of immediately. Your plane is now boarding—you better get on. We're sorry for the inconvenience."

It's amazing how stupid and senseless some people are. Regretfully you board the plane. As you travel home, you have to fight back the tears. A great scientific discovery is lost—an alien creature has senselessly died, and what happened to you on Hawk Mountain remains a mystery that may never be solved.

The End

When the police arrive, they are followed by a van from the ASPCA. Moments later, you're showing them Slimy's cage. The men just stand there dumbfounded. It's obvious they don't know what to make of this creature. You can't blame them any.

"We'll take it into custody," the officer says, "but we don't have any place to keep dogs and cats, much less aliens from outer space. The ASPCA here will have to take care of it until we figure out what to do. We'll wait for further instructions and let you know what happens."

As the ASPCA load the cage into the van, you explain Slimy's special diet to them. "Take good care of it," you say.

You feel sad watching the van pull away.

Back home a few days later, you phone the ASPCA office to find out how Slimy is doing. Your heart sinks as you hear the bad news—Slimy died the day before. The people at the shelter gave him fish, vegetables, fruits, and baby food. No one could believe that he only liked used motor oil and battery acid.

The End

110

You decide to call Professor Burns for advice, but you're unable to reach him. His secretary tells you that he won't be back for a week. Unfortunately, your stay at the ranch will be over by then. You'll just have to take the capsule back home with you.

The following Saturday your uncle Howard and your aunt Nan take you to the airport. You promise them you'll write and let them know what happens with your capsule.

As you prepare to board your plane, you're surprised to see a number of policemen and security guards all over the place. One guard tells you that there's been a bomb threat and that all the packages will have to be searched, as well as X-rayed.

You take off your backpack and open it up for inspection. The security guard removes the capsule and examines it curiously. He motions toward a policeman. "Hey, look at this."

The officer takes the capsule and holds it up to the light, then to his ear. "I saw a bomb that looked like this once," he said. "What, exactly, is in here?"

Go on to the next page.

"I'm not sure," you say, "but I think it could be an alien life-form."

The security guard pulls out a jackknife and snaps it open. "I'll get to the bottom of this," he says.

"No, don't!" you say, trying to grab the capsule away from him.

The policeman swiftly stops you. "Look, kid, either we open it here or we turn it over to the bomb squad."

Turn to page 86.

112

You follow Professor Burns through the entrance, only to be startled at the weird sight before you. At least half of the lab is occupied by a large aquarium, enclosed behind heavy glass panels. In the smoggy interior, Slimy crouches next to a pile of oily rags and waste refuse. His two trunklike appendages are folded in front of him, the way a human might fold his arms.

You can't believe what you're seeing—he's watching a television set, and he's holding a remote control in one of his trunks. Several scientists are standing by, observing. Some of them are making entries on their laptop computers. A video camera is recording the whole scene.

"One would be inclined to believe that any creature that looks like Slimy must be stupid," Professor Burns says. "But from our observations, it's our belief that he's just as intelligent as we are."

"This is amazing," you say, "but what were you saying about an alien invasion?"

The expression on Professor Burns's face turns grave. "During the past few weeks we've received a number of reports involving memory loss from victims throughout the United States who've had experiences similar to yours. There have been reports from Eureka Springs, Arkansas, and just this morning we received one from Everglades National Park in Florida. It's only speculation, but we think the power domes may be planting capsules, or eggs, from which aliens like Slimy will one day hatch. We can't be sure, but there may already be hundreds of domes planted around the world."

Turn to page 91.

114

You back up to your tent and fix your eyes on the glowing dome.

"Maybe we should back up even farther," Derek says.

You're about to say that you agree with him, but you suddenly feel too dizzy to talk. The next moment everything turns black. A thousand stars are now shining in the sky.

"Is everyone all right?" Professor Burns says.

"I'm okay, Dad," Derek says.

"Me, too," you add.

"Well, we all know what happened," Professor Burns says. "We experienced memory loss, for at least six hours, it would appear. It's nighttime now."

"We also lost Slimy," you say. "He's nowhere in sight. And neither is the power dome."

"Yes, I'm afraid we'll never see our alien friend again," the professor says. "And without him, we may never solve the mystery of the power dome."

The End

ABOUT THE AUTHOR

EDWARD PACKARD is a graduate of Princeton University and Columbia Law School. He developed the unique storytelling approach used in the Choose Your Own Adventure series while thinking up stories for his children, Caroline, Andrea, and Wells.

ABOUT THE ILLUSTRATOR

FRANK BOLLE studied at Pratt Institute. He has worked as an illustrator for many national magazines and now creates and draws cartoons for magazines as well. He has also worked in advertising and children's educational materials and has drawn and collaborated on several newspaper comic strips, including *Annie* and *Winnie Winkle*. Most recently he has illustrated *The Case of the Silk King, Longhorn Territory, Track of the Bear, Master of Kung Fu, South Pole Sabotage, Return of the Ninja, You Are a Genius, Through the Black Hole, The Worst Day of Your Life, Master of Tae Kwon Do, The Cobra Connection, Hijacked!,* and *Master of Karate* in the Choose Your Own Adventure series. A native of Brooklyn Heights, New York, Mr. Bolle now lives and works in Westport, Connecticut.